# Princess Caitlin's Tiara

Written by
Kim Messinger and Michael LaLumiere

Illustrated by Ginger Nielson

Stagger Lee Books
San Francisco

ISBN-978-1-4116-0926-6

For Laura and Caitlin

And in memory of their

Poppa Lou

    Caitlin sat glumly at the kitchen table watching raindrops roll down the window pane. With a flick of a finger she sent a toast crumb whizzing across the kitchen. The tiny crumb-turned-missile whistled right by her mother's ear as she walked through the kitchen door carrying a basket of laundry.

"Watch out, Momma. I'm in a big old bad news funk!"

Momma studied her scowling daughter. She pulled a fluffy, purple sweater from her basket.

"Here, put this on, Sweet Potato. You always say it makes you feel SOOOOOOO GOOOOOOOD, like a princess."

Thunder rumbled outside. Caitlin buried her head in her arms and groaned.

"Not even that sweater can make me feel like a princess today, Momma. I told you. This is a big old funk. A humongous funk. A funk that could eat Chicago."

"Well, when I was a little girl I had something that made me feel like a princess. It didn't matter if it was raining, or if I knew my mother was cooking liver for dinner, or even if your Uncle Bobby had just dunked my Barbie in the toilet. All I had to do was wear my beautiful princess tiara, and the rain instantly turned into sunshine. I became funk-proof."

"Do you still have that tiara, Momma? I really need it BAD."

"Oh, it's around here somewhere. But my tiara won't fit you. You have to make your own, Sweet Potato."

"OK, Momma. I'm so desperate I'll try anything!" Caitlin ran up and down the stairs, yanking open drawers, filling a box with what she needed. She imagined her mother as a princess with a beautiful tiara in her long curly hair. And even though she was in a funk--and she knew you aren't supposed to laugh when you're in a funk-- Caitlin giggled right out loud.

First, Caitlin cut a long, narrow strip of poster board and stapled the two ends together so it made a circle the size of her head. She wrapped silver foil round and round till the band shimmered when she held it up under the kitchen light.

"With this shiny tiara I can snowboard down steep snowy hills at the
South Pole, even in the dark! A thousand penguins will see me sparkling
in the moonlight and chase me for miles trying to catch up. I can climb
the tallest mountains in the world. All the other climbers will call and
say, 'Please invite us on your next expedition. With your dazzling tiara, you
can lead the way through even the worst storm.' "

"I'll glue on some blue ribbon next. It's the color of the ocean. I'm sure it will make my tiara waterproof! I'll be able to dive deep with the mermaids and the whales. A sea horse will offer me a ride and show me sunken treasure chests filled with rubies and emeralds and pearls. I'll play 'Go Fish' with a grumpy old octopus and always win."

Caitlin practiced her backstroke around
the kitchen, then stopped and bent three yellow
pipe cleaners into diamonds and attached them to the front of the
tiara. She squirted the diamonds with sticky glue and sprinkled on
sparkly glitter. She carefully nestled the tiara in her hair and
smiled at her reflection in the kitchen window.

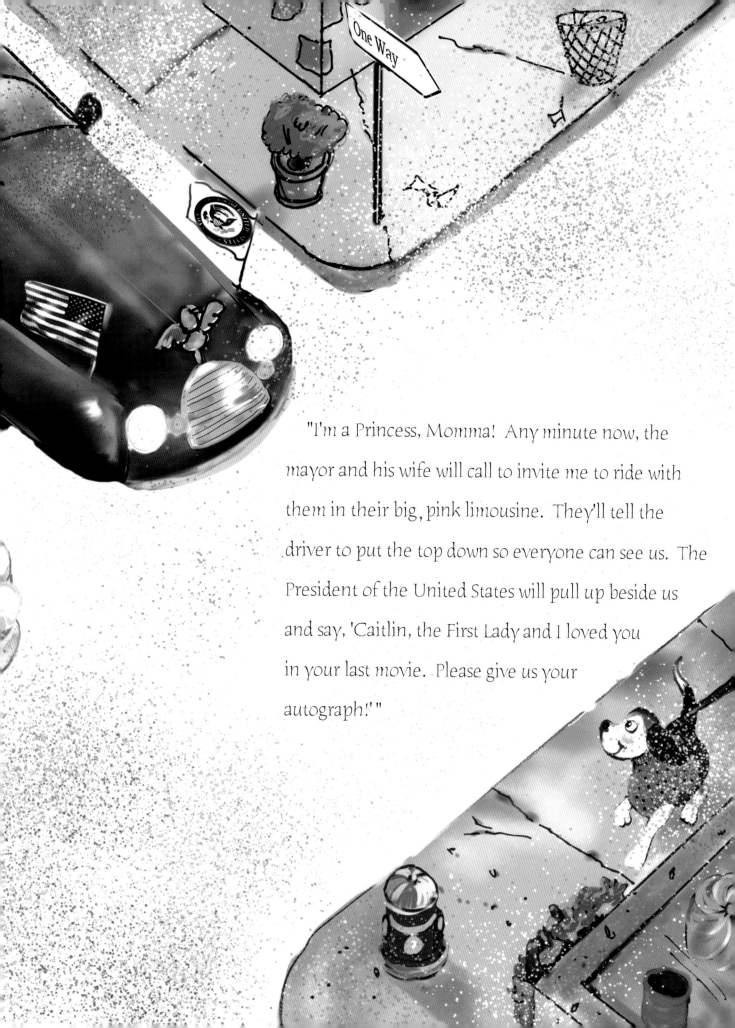

"I'm a Princess, Momma! Any minute now, the mayor and his wife will call to invite me to ride with them in their big, pink limousine. They'll tell the driver to put the top down so everyone can see us. The President of the United States will pull up beside us and say, 'Caitlin, the First Lady and I loved you in your last movie. Please give us your autograph!'"

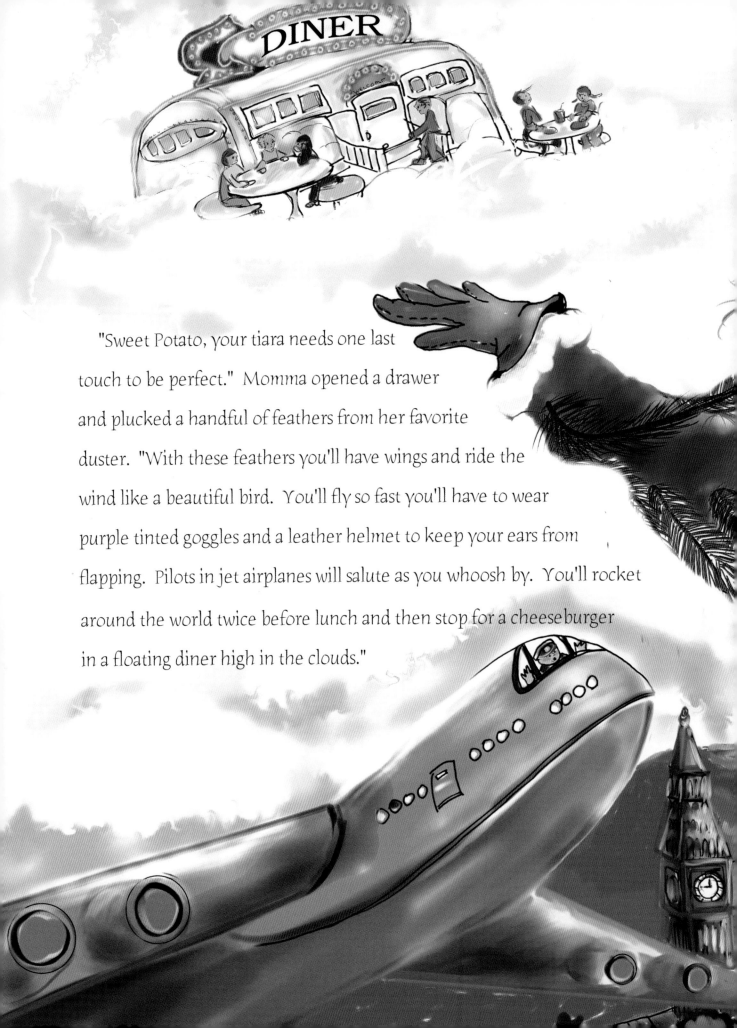

"Sweet Potato, your tiara needs one last touch to be perfect." Momma opened a drawer and plucked a handful of feathers from her favorite duster. "With these feathers you'll have wings and ride the wind like a beautiful bird. You'll fly so fast you'll have to wear purple tinted goggles and a leather helmet to keep your ears from flapping. Pilots in jet airplanes will salute as you whoosh by. You'll rocket around the world twice before lunch and then stop for a cheeseburger in a floating diner high in the clouds."

"It's splendiferous, Momma!  I'll
challenge Superman to a race to Paris, France.
He'll probably turn back half way there.
He'll say, 'You go too fast, Caitlin, and I'm
tired.'  But I'll keep going.  As I glide by
Notre Dame even the grumpiest gargoyles
will smile and wave their paws.  Parisian pigeons
wearing little berets will coo ooh-la-la and want
me to share a baguette with them on top of
the Eiffel Tower."

"Well, Sweet Potato, how's that big old bad news funk doing now?"

"Princesses don't have time to be in a funk!" said Caitlin as she ran up the stairs to her room. She was in a hurry to show her new tiara to Beany Black Bear, Joy the Giraffe and Mr. Monkey. And to maybe peek once or twice in the mirror.

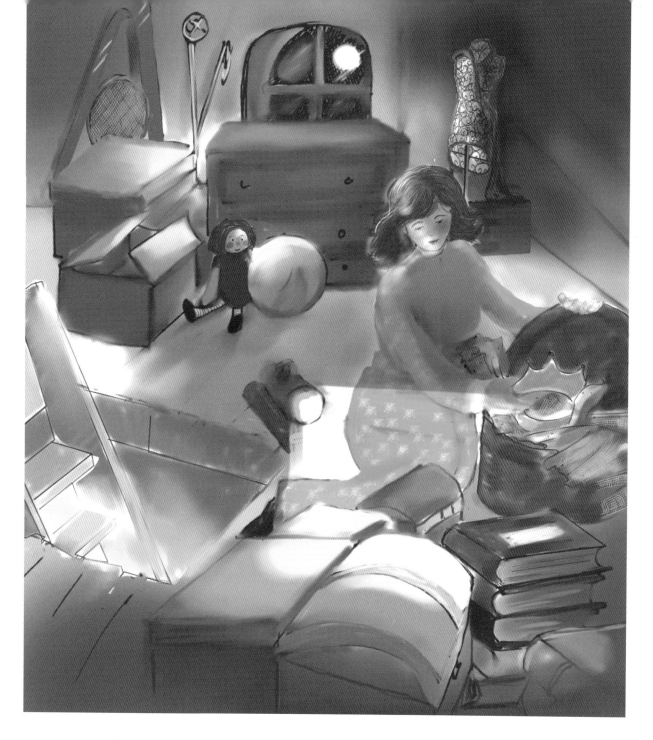

After dinner that night, Momma found a flashlight and
climbed the stairs into the attic. In a far corner she
opened a hat box covered in tattered, dusty silk. She
pushed aside crinkly tissue paper and carefully
lifted out the tiara she had worn when she was a little
girl. A lot of glitter was missing. The diamonds were
squished. But the tiara still fit.

Momma knocked on Caitlin's door. "Is it safe to tuck you into bed, Sweet Potato? Are there any missiles flying around in there or funks lurking in the closet?"

Caitlin giggled. "I'm a Princess, Momma, and I'm having tea with the Queen of England. There's not a funk in sight."

Caitlin jumped up from her tea party and almost dropped her tiny, violet covered cup when she saw Momma. "WOW! You found YOUR tiara. It's beautiful. Do you feel like a princess?"

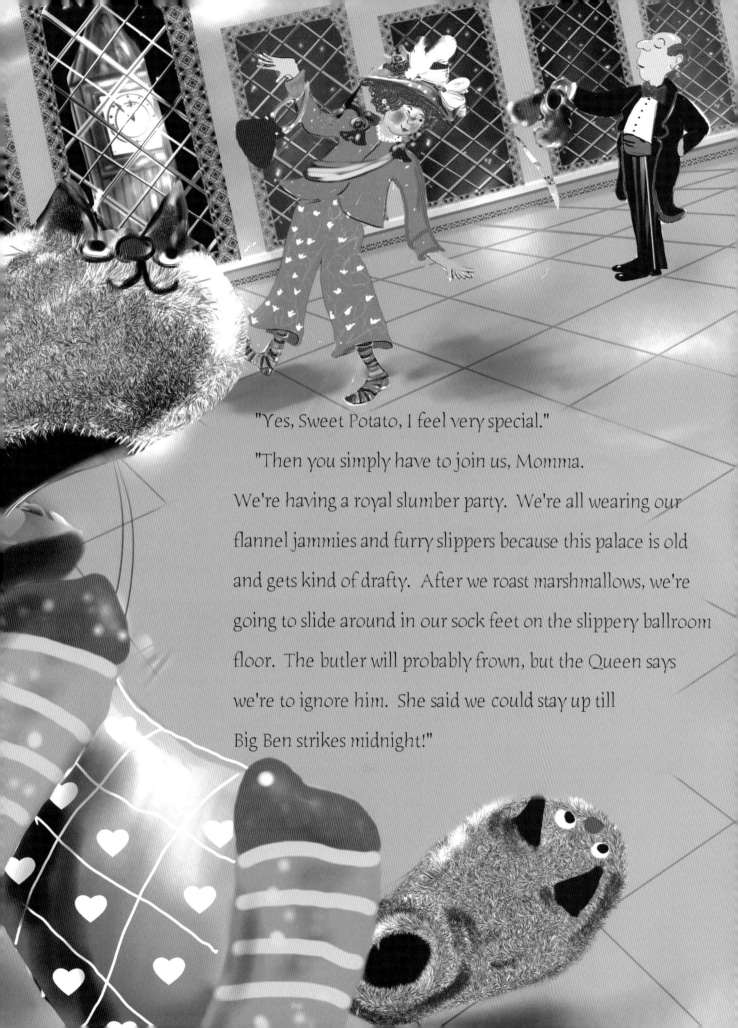

"Yes, Sweet Potato, I feel very special."

"Then you simply have to join us, Momma.
We're having a royal slumber party. We're all wearing our
flannel jammies and furry slippers because this palace is old
and gets kind of drafty. After we roast marshmallows, we're
going to slide around in our sock feet on the slippery ballroom
floor. The butler will probably frown, but the Queen says
we're to ignore him. She said we could stay up till
Big Ben strikes midnight!"

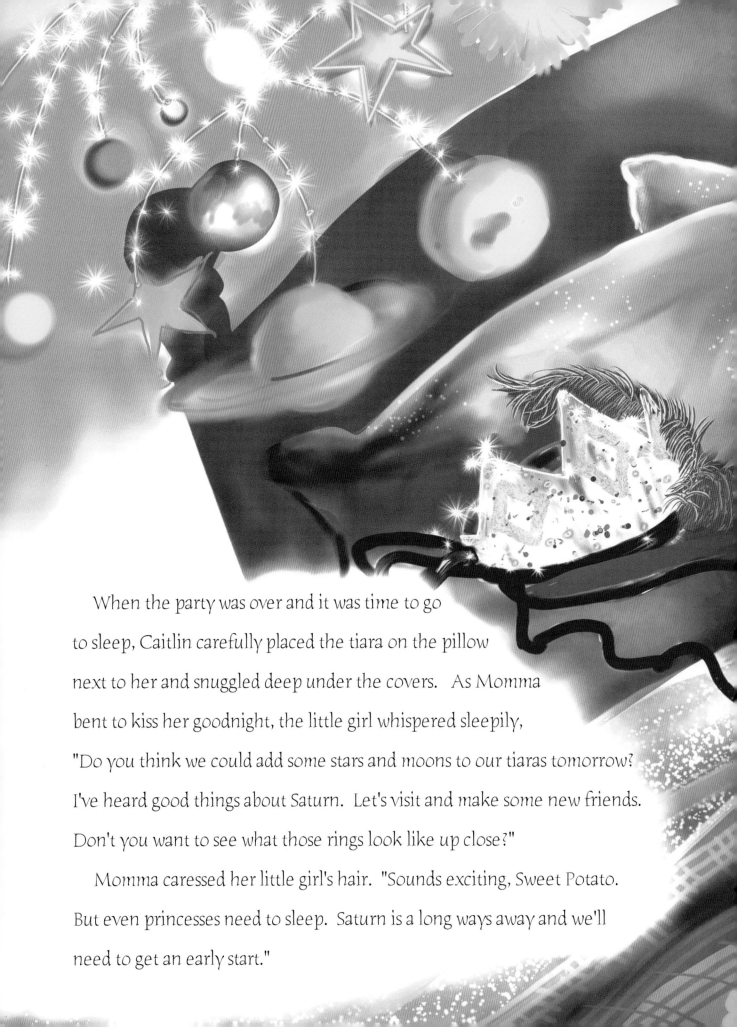

When the party was over and it was time to go
to sleep, Caitlin carefully placed the tiara on the pillow
next to her and snuggled deep under the covers.  As Momma
bent to kiss her goodnight, the little girl whispered sleepily,
"Do you think we could add some stars and moons to our tiaras tomorrow?
I've heard good things about Saturn.  Let's visit and make some new friends.
Don't you want to see what those rings look like up close?"

Momma caressed her little girl's hair.  "Sounds exciting, Sweet Potato.
But even princesses need to sleep.  Saturn is a long ways away and we'll
need to get an early start."